UNCLE ELEPHANT

BY ARNOLD LOBEL

An I CAN READ Book ®

HarperCollinsPublishers

For Charlotte Zolotow

HarperCollins®, ☐®, and I Can Read Book® are trademarks
of HarperCollins Publishers Inc.

Uncle Elephant

Library of Congress Cataloging-in-Publication data
Lobel, Arnold.
    Uncle Elephant.

    (An I can read book)
    Summary: Uncle Elephant comes to the rescue when his
nephew's parents are lost at sea and cares for him until
they are found again.
    [1. Elephants—Fiction. 2. Uncles—Fiction]
I. Title. II. Series: I can read book.
PZ7.L7795Un 1981   [E]   80-8944
ISBN 0-06-023979-4   AACR2
ISBN 0-06-023980-8 (lib. bdg.)

UNCLE
ELEPHANT

CONTENTS

Uncle Elephant Opens the Door

Mother and Father

went for a sail

in their boat.

I could not go with them.

I had a runny trunk

and a sore throat.

I went home to bed.

6

There was a storm.

The boat did not come back.

Mother and Father

were missing at sea.

I was alone.

I sat in my room

with the curtains closed.

I heard my door opening.

"Hello, I am your Uncle Elephant,"
said a voice.

I looked at Uncle Elephant.

"What are you staring at?"
he asked.

"Ah, I know,

you are looking at my wrinkles."

"You *do* have many wrinkles,"
I said.

"Yes," said Uncle Elephant,

"I have more wrinkles

than a tree has leaves.

I have more wrinkles

than a beach has sand.

I have more wrinkles

than the sky has stars."

9

"Why do you have
so many wrinkles?" I asked.
"Because I am old,"
said Uncle Elephant.
"Now come out
of this dark place."
"Where will I go?" I asked.
"Come and visit me,"
said Uncle Elephant.

Uncle Elephant Counts the Poles

I sat

with Uncle Elephant

on the train.

We shared

a bag of peanuts.

We looked

out of the window.

The country

rushed past.

"One, two, three.

Oh, I missed one,"

said Uncle Elephant.

"What are you counting?"

I asked.

"I am trying to count

the houses

as they go by," he said.

12

"One, two, three, four.

I missed one again,"

said Uncle Elephant.

"What are you counting?"

I asked.

13

"I am trying to count

the fields

as they go by,"

he said.

14

"One, two, three, four, five.

I missed another one,"

said Uncle Elephant.

"What are you counting now?"

I asked.

"I am trying to count

the telephone poles

as they go by.

But everything is passing

too darn fast,"

said Uncle Elephant.

Uncle Elephant was right.

Everything *was* passing very fast.

"One, two, three,

four, five,

six, seven, eight,

nine, and ten!"

said Uncle Elephant.

"What are you counting

this time?"

I asked.

"I am counting

the peanut shells,"

said Uncle Elephant.

"They are easier to count.

16

They are all

in one place.

They are all

sitting on your lap."

17

The train raced along.

We finished

the whole bag of peanuts.

There were

many more shells

for Uncle Elephant

to count.

Uncle Elephant Lights a Lamp

We came to

Uncle Elephant's house.

"We will light a lamp

and have some supper,"

said Uncle Elephant.

He took a lamp

from the shelf and lit it.

"Hey there!"

said a small voice

from inside the lamp.

"Did you hear that?"

asked Uncle Elephant.

"This lamp can talk!"

"It is a magic lamp!" I said.

"Then we can make wishes!"

said Uncle Elephant.

"I wish for an airplane

that I can fly myself,"

I said.

"I wish for a polka-dot suit
with striped pants,"
said Uncle Elephant.
"I wish for a banana split
with ten scoops
of ice cream," I said.

"I wish for a box filled
with one hundred big cigars,"
said Uncle Elephant.

We rubbed the lamp.

We sat and waited.

A little spider

crawled out.

"I wish

that you would

turn off this lamp

and leave me

in peace,"

said the spider.

"I live in there.

It is getting hot."

Uncle Elephant made

the spider's wish

come true.

He was happy

to turn off the lamp.

23

Uncle Elephant

put the lamp

back on the shelf.

We ate our supper

by the light

of the moon.

Uncle Elephant Trumpets the Dawn

"VOOMAROOOM!"

It was morning.

I heard

a noise outside.

I ran to the window.

Uncle Elephant

was standing in the garden.

His ears flapped

in the breeze.

He raised his trunk.

"VOOMAROOOM!"

trumpeted Uncle Elephant.

"What are you doing?"

I asked.

"I always
welcome the dawn this way,"
said Uncle Elephant.
"Every new day
deserves a good,
loud trumpet."

27

"I have planted

all these flowers myself.

Come outside

and let me introduce you

to everyone,"

said Uncle Elephant.

"Roses, daisies,

daffodils and marigolds,

I want you

to meet my nephew."

I bowed to the flowers.

Uncle Elephant

was pleased.

"This garden

is my favorite place

in the world,"

said Uncle Elephant.

"It is

my own kingdom."

"If this is your kingdom,"

I said,

"are you the king?"

"I suppose I am,"

said Uncle Elephant.

"If you are the king,"

I said,

"I must be the prince."

"Of course,"

said Uncle Elephant,

"you *must* be the prince!"

We made ourselves

crowns of flowers.

Uncle Elephant raised his trunk.

"VOOMAROOOM!"

I raised my trunk.

"VOOMAROOOM!"

We were the king

and the prince.

We were trumpeting the dawn.

Uncle Elephant Feels the Creaks

Uncle Elephant

and I

went for a walk.

"Ouch!"

cried Uncle Elephant.

"What is the matter?"

I asked.

"I am feeling the creaks,"

said Uncle Elephant.

"What are the creaks?"

I asked.

"Sometimes they happen

to old elephants like me,"

he said.

"My back creaks,

my knees creak,

my feet creak,

even my trunk creaks.

The creaks

are quite uncomfortable."

We walked slowly home.

Uncle Elephant

sat down carefully

in his softest chair.

"Ah," he said,

"the creaks in the bottom

part of me are gone."

Uncle Elephant

rested his head

on the back of the chair.

"Ah," he said,

"the creaks in the top

part of me are gone."

Uncle Elephant

put his legs on a footstool.

"Ah," he said.

"The creaks in my feet

are gone."

"Are you feeling better?"

I asked.

"Almost,"

said Uncle Elephant.

"If you let me

tell you a story,

I am sure all of my creaks

will go away."

Uncle Elephant Tells a Story

"Once there was

a King and a Prince,"

said Uncle Elephant.

"The Prince was brave.

He was young and smart.

The King was old.

He had many wrinkles.

"They lived in a castle

at the edge of a woods.

One day the King

and the Prince

went for a walk.

They became lost

in the woods.

'Oh, help!'

cried the King.

'Do not worry,'

said the Prince.

'We will

find our way home.'

" 'Oh, help and ouch!'

cried the King.

'I am tired.

I am creaking all over.

I want to go home.

I want to sit in my chair.'

"They wandered

in circles for hours.

They could not

find their castle.

A lion jumped out at them.

'A king and a prince!

Just what I want for dinner!'

roared the lion.

"He showed them his sharp teeth.

The King and the Prince

raised their trunks.

'VOOMAROOOM!'

They both trumpeted

as loudly as they could.

The lion was so afraid

that every one of his teeth

popped out.

He ran away.

"The King tried to look

over the tops of the trees.

'My old eyes are weak,'

he said.

'I can't see a darn thing.'

'King,' said the Prince,

'my eyes are sharp.

Lift me up on your head.'

The King lifted the Prince.

"The Prince looked

over the tops of the trees.

'There it is!' he cried.

'I can see the tower

of our castle.

Now we are not lost!'

"And that," said Uncle Elephant,

"was how the King and the Prince

helped each other

to find their way home."

Uncle Elephant had ended his story.

"There," he said, "that does it.

From top to bottom

I do not feel a single creak!"

Uncle Elephant Wears His Clothes

There was a picture

in Uncle Elephant's

living room.

"That is a picture of me

when I was your age,"

said Uncle Elephant.

I looked at the picture.

45

Uncle Elephant

was with

his mother and father.

They looked

just like mine.

I felt sad.

I began to cry.

Uncle Elephant looked sad too.

"Now, now," he said,

"let's not have

any of this.

I must do something

to make us happy.

"I will wear

some funny clothes.

That will make us smile."

Uncle Elephant

opened his closet door.

He looked at his hats

and his ties and his shirts

and his pants and his jackets.

"My clothes are not funny,"

said Uncle Elephant.

"What can I do?"

Uncle Elephant

went into his closet.

In a while he came out.

He was wearing

all of his hats, all of his ties,

all of his shirts, all of his pants,

and all of his jackets.

Uncle Elephant

was wearing everything

on top of everything.

49

Uncle Elephant

was a pile of clothes

with two big ears.

First I smiled.

Then I giggled.

Then I laughed.

We both laughed so hard,

we forgot to feel sad.

Uncle Elephant Writes a Song

"Sing a song for me,"

said Uncle Elephant.

"I don't know any songs,"

I said.

"Not one?"

asked Uncle Elephant.

"Not even one," I said.

"Then I will write you
a song of your own,"
said Uncle Elephant.
He wrote the words
of the song
on a piece of paper.

"I have a song.

It's an elephant song.

I will sing it

whenever I please.

With my trunk in a loop,

I will sing while I swoop

from the vines

and the branches of trees.

53

"I have a song.

It's an elephant song.

I will sing it

wherever I go.

Upside down on my head,

with my ears as a sled,

I will sing

as I slide through the snow.

"I have a song.

It's an elephant song.

I will sing it

whatever I do.

When I sing while I munch

on my peanutty lunch,

I will not miss a note

as I chew.

55

"I have a song.

It's an elephant song.

I will sing it

and never forget

that, of all music played,

there is no better made

than an uncle

and nephew duet."

Uncle Elephant

made up a tune

to go with

the words.

Together, we sang

my song.

We sang it

over and over.

Uncle Elephant Closes the Door

One day a telegram came

to Uncle Elephant's house.

It was from

my mother and father!

They had been

found and rescued.

They were alive!

Uncle Elephant

and I

danced for joy.

"I must take you home

at once," he said.

I sat

with Uncle Elephant

on the train.

We looked

out of the window.

"One, two, three, four..."

said Uncle Elephant.

"Are you counting the houses?"

I asked.

"No," said Uncle Elephant.

"Are you counting the fields?"

I asked.

"No," said Uncle Elephant.

"I know," I said.

"You are counting

the telephone poles."

"No,"

said Uncle Elephant.

"Not this time."

Mother and Father

were waiting for us.

I rushed into their arms.

That night,

after a fine dinner,

I sang my song.

Uncle Elephant

played the piano.

Before I fell asleep,

Uncle Elephant came into my room.

"Do you want to know what I was

counting on the train?" he asked.

"Yes," I said.

"I was counting days,"

said Uncle Elephant.

"The days we spent together?"

I asked.

"Yes," said Uncle Elephant.

"They were wonderful days.

They all passed too fast."

We promised

to see each other often.

Uncle Elephant

kissed me

good night

and closed

the door.

DISCARD

DATE			